Planet Robonica

by Alison Reynolds

illustrated by Alan Brown

a Capstone company — publishers for children

Engage Literacy is published in the UK by Raintree.
Raintree is an imprint of Capstone Global Library Limited, a company
incorporated in England and Wales having its registered office at 264 Banbury
Road, Oxford, OX2 7DY – Registered company number: 6695582

www.raintree.co.uk

10 9 8 7 6 5 4 3 2 1
Printed and bound in China.

Planet Robonica
ISBN: 978-1-4747-1792-2

Contents

Chapter 1

Astrolab

The hairs on Max's neck stood up. He turned around and jumped. A tall, silver robot silently looked down at him and his best friend, Jack.

"This school trip to Astrolab is turning out to be kind of strange," Jack whispered.

Max nodded. Robots didn't usually make Max Jupiter Astro Marriot nervous. He was a secret Space Guard, like his parents. They helped to protect Planet Earth from danger.

The robot pointed down the long hall.

Jack shook his head and looked back at their teacher. "Mr Sona will be angry if we wander off," he said.

"We can sneak back in a few minutes," said Max as he gripped Jack's arm. He pulled Jack down the hall, after the speeding robot.

They stopped at a gleaming red door with a sign:

CAUTION: FLIGHT SIMULATOR

"What's this?" asked Jack.

"It's a machine that shows what it's like to fly through space," explained Max.

Chapter 2

Blast off!

The tall robot grabbed the boys as the door swished open and he pushed them inside.

Jack rubbed his back. "Ouch!" he said. "Why so pushy?"

"I did not mean to hurt you, but I am in a hurry," the robot responded.

The room's walls glowed with a soft, blue light.

Max rushed over to a platform. "Is this a teleporter?"

"Correct. It will take you wherever you need to go." The robot glided across to the control panel and pressed a big, black button.

A metallic voice said, "Countdown has started: 10... 9..."

"Cool," Jack said. "We're getting the entire space-flight experience."

The spaceship trembled as if the motors had started.

"8... 7..."

Max looked around the simulator with surprise. "I've been in Earth spaceships before, and this is unlike any I've ever seen!"

"Correct," said the robot. "It is able to do much more than an Earth spaceship."

"6... 5..."

"Jack, let's get out of here!" yelled Max, and they ran towards the door.

"4... 3..."

A large net dropped from the ceiling. The boys were instantly trapped.

"You are not going anywhere," the robot said.

"2..."

The boys struggled to get free of the net, but it was hopeless.

"1... Blast off!"

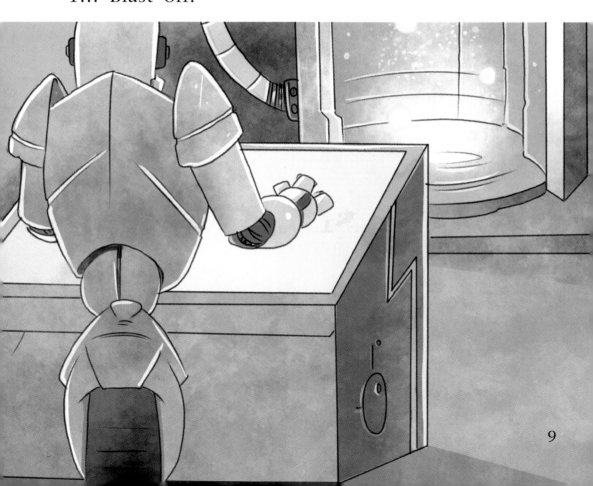

Chapter 3

Planet Robonica

Max looked down at his GPS, trying to find out their location. But his GPS couldn't pick up a signal and tell him where they were. "Where are we?"

"In the Asteroid Belt," the robot answered.

Jack looked nervous.

"Scientists say the odds of hitting an asteroid in the belt are one in a billion," Max said. He was trying to make his friend less afraid.

"Correct," the robot said. "Max Marriot, my data about you is true. You are very clever."

"How do you know my name?" asked Max.

"Full name, Max Jupiter Astro Marriot. And you may call me Robot X."

A metallic voice said, "Prepare for Mega-twist Drive."

"What's that?" shouted Jack.

"It means we're going to travel faster than the speed of light," answered Max.

"Correct," said Robot X.

The spaceship started to spin. Max shut his eyes and wished he hadn't eaten that extra banana pancake for breakfast. His stomach hurt from all the spinning.

"Destination reached," said Robot X.

Max opened his eyes. He tried again to get a signal on his GPS. "Now where are we?"

The net slowly lifted off the boys. A huge screen lowered from the ceiling. It showed a large map of the galaxy with a glowing circle in the centre.

"My home, the planet Robonica," said Robot X, pointing at the screen.

Suddenly, hundreds of robots appeared on the screen. They were different shapes and sizes. Some were tall, and others were the size of bowling balls. They were gathered in front of a large, empty stage. To the right of the stage was a strange orange building.

Max gulped. "Why are we here?"

Robot X's head turned to stare at Max. "Why? You must help me with my mission."

Chapter 4

The mission

"What mission?" shouted Max and Jack.

"I need the help of a Space Guard to save my planet."

"You've got a wire loose," said Jack. "We're not Space Guards."

Max's face reddened. "Actually, I am," he admitted.

"I thought we were best friends," said Jack, looking hurt. "No secrets."

"It's not just my secret," said Max. "My parents and I are part of a secret group responsible for protecting Planet Earth. We're still best friends, Jack. I'm sorry you got dragged into this. Robot X, I'm only 10. Why didn't you choose a Space Guard with more experience?"

"My data shows that you are the Space Guard most likely to help me. You are too young to have formed fixed ideas about robots. Many people think we are just faceless metal objects," Robot X explained.

"What's the problem?" Max asked.

"The Ruler is destroying my planet's robots. He has them taken apart and sold for scrap metal. He calls Robonica a scrap yard."

Max looked at the screen. "Why don't all the robots just attack the Ruler?"

"The Ruler has a robot control machine. The robots are totally under his power. I need you to find and destroy the machine. If you succeed, the robots will be freed from the Ruler's control."

Max looked at Jack. "Are you in?"

Jack nodded. "I'm in!"

The two boys high-fived each other.

Chapter 5

Vile-Tron

"One problem," said Robot X.

"You can't come with us," Max guessed.

"Correct," said Robot X. "I was away on a space flight when the Ruler took control. If I land on Robonica, I may come under the Ruler's power. You will have to use the teleporter to get to Robonica without me."

Jack pointed at the screen. "What's *that*?" he asked. A huge robot wearing a gas mask suddenly appeared on the stage.

"That is Vile-Tron, the Ruler," said Robot X. "He is the most evil alien in the universe. He was made from dirt mixed with a very strong metal. The mixture smells terrible so he stinks, too."

The robots raised their arms in the air and cheered Vile-Tron. Two orange robots glided beside him.

"Time to collect scrap metal!" Vile-Tron boomed.

The robots formed a line and slowly began entering the orange building. After about 20 of the robots were inside, Vile-Tron held up an arm and yelled, "Enough!" The robots outside the building stopped. The two orange robots glided into the building. A short while later they left, carrying stacks of metal in their arms.

Robot X, Max and Jack watched the screen in silence as the orange robots loaded the metal into a spaceship. The robots made a few more back-and-forth trips until the spaceship was full. Vile-Tron nodded and then waved the spaceship away. He stepped onto a teleporter, pressed a button on his belt and disappeared.

Max looked away from the screen. "If we're going to get past the Ruler, we'll need to look like robots."

"Correct," responded Robot X. He pointed to the screen that was now displaying a large map of Planet Robonica. "According to the map, you'll need to teleport to the stage, right about here. My data shows that Vile-Tron hides the control system there."

Jack pointed to the orange building on the map. "We're staying far away from this place!"

"Correct," said Robot X. The robot opened a cupboard and pulled out two robot shells.

When the boys climbed into the shells, the metal tightened and moulded to their bodies.

"Cool!" said Jack, gliding around the control room.

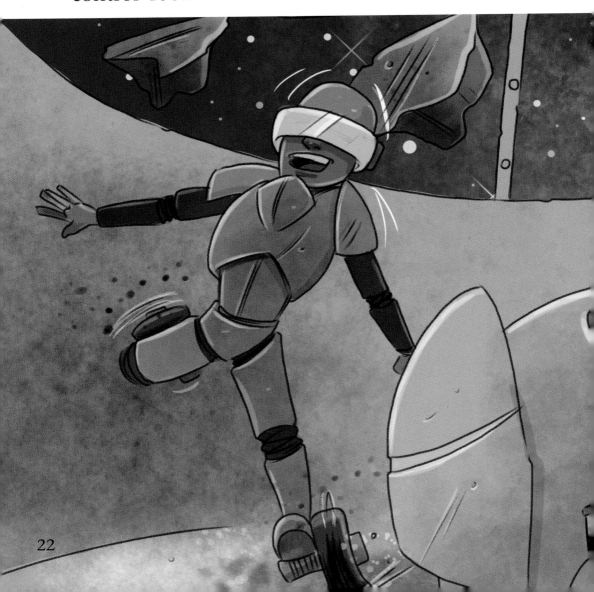

"We'll do our best," Max promised Robot X.

"Correct," said Robot X quietly.

Max and Jack stood together on the teleporter.

"Well, here goes!" said Max.

"3... 2... 1... READY!" they shouted.

Chapter 6

Save Robonica!

Max and Jack were standing on Robonica's stage. Hundreds of robots were gathered below them.

"Look!" Jack pointed to a small hole in the stage floor. "That looks like a trapdoor."

Max tried to open it, but it was locked. A siren began screeching.

"This must be Vile-Tron's control system, Jack!"

"We've got to get off the stage, Max!"

He and Max rolled down a ramp off the stage. The teleporter buzzed, and Vile-Tron appeared once again as the siren stopped.

Vile-Tron frowned. "Which one of you useless metal dustbins touched my stage? File up here, one at a time. I want to take a close look at each of you."

Robot after robot glided up the ramp. Vile-Tron stared at each one, then waved it on. Only Max and Jack were left. It was Jack's turn. Vile-Tron peered into his visor, then waved him away, too.

Max took his turn. While standing in front of Vile-Tron, Max noticed two things. Vile-Tron smelled terrible, and he had a silver key hanging off his belt.

"Pile of scrap!" shouted Vile-Tron, giving Max a swift kick.

Before Max tipped over, he reached out and grabbed the key. He did it so quickly that Vile-Tron didn't even notice. Max's robot helmet fell off as he hit the stage.

"An Earthling!" screamed Vile-Tron. "*You* were touching my robot control system."

He pointed to Jack. "Robot, destroy this human!"

Jack slowly glided up the ramp.

"You must be the slowest robot in the universe," grumbled Vile-Tron. "Hurry up!"

Max quietly crawled to the trapdoor and unlocked it with the key. He threw the door open and saw a panel with shiny buttons and flashing lights. Vile-Tron was too busy watching Jack to notice.

Jack walked over to Max with his arm raised. While bringing his arm down, Jack suddenly swung around and pushed Vile-Tron off the stage.

Vile-Tron roared, "Robots! Catch them and attack!"

The robots below the stage looked up at the boys and started walking towards the ramp.

"Hurry, Max!" shouted Jack.

Max looked up at Jack, flashed a grin, then smashed his fist into the robot control machine.

A loud robotic wail filled the air as all the robots got their memories back.

Vile-Tron tried to climb onto the stage, but the crowd of angry robots yanked him back.

"They're taking Vile-Tron apart!" gasped Jack.

"Let's get out of here!" yelled Max.

"Run!" shouted Jack.

Max and Jack raced across the stage and leaped onto the teleporter.

"Back to Robot X!" they shouted.

Chapter 7

Home

"Robonica is a crazy place," said Jack.

"Correct," replied Robot X.

Max and Jack were celebrating their success with a feast of dried space food. Robot X had happily prepared it for them.

"You will both be welcomed to Planet Robonica as heroes. I will explain to the robots that you two saved them," said Robot X proudly.

"Cool!" said Max and Jack between bites of dried space pizza.

"We'd better start thinking about what we're going to tell Mr Sona," said Max.

"We have only been away for 10 Earth minutes," Robot X explained. "Your teacher may not have noticed you are missing."

"Wow!" said Jack. "Time sure flies in space."

"Correct. Especially when I use the Mega-twist Drive." Robot X called up the spaceship's GPS. "Do you have time for another adventure, my friends?"

"We've got time, don't we, Max?" Jack asked.

"Correct!" laughed Space Guard Max Jupiter Astro Marriot.